This book belongs to...

PE'NNY

gym giraffe

Written by Ronne Randall
Illustrated by Jacqueline East

Bright ☆ Sparks

Jeremy Giraffe loved going out with his dad to gather juicy green leaves for dinner.

"This is where you find the most delicious leaves, Jeremy," said Dad, reaching wa-a-a-y up to a very high branch. "Remember — the tallest trees have the tastiest leaves, and the tiny top leaves are the tenderest!"

One morning, Jeremy decided it was time he went out to gather leaves on his own.

"The tallest trees have the tastiest leaves," he whispered to himself as he trotted along, "and the tiny top leaves are the tenderest."

Jeremy stopped at the tallest tree he could find, and looked up. Sure enough, right at the top, there were some tiny, tender leaves just waiting to be plucked.

stre-e-e-e-etching

his neck just as he had seen his dad do, Jeremy reached
as high as he could — it wasn't very high!

"Oh, dear," he thought. "How will I ever
reach the tastiest, tenderest, tiny top
leaves if my neck won't stretch?"

So Jeremy went back home with his neck hanging down in despair.

"Why, Jeremy, whatever is the matter?" asked his mom. When Jeremy told her, she gave his neck a nuzzle.

"You're still growing," she assured him. "Just eat your greens and get lots of sleep, and your neck will soon be long enough to reach the tastiest, tiniest, tenderest leaves on the tallest tree tops in the jungle!"

Jeremy couldn't wait for his neck to grow. That afternoon, he rushed out to try again.

High above him, Portia Parrot saw Jeremy struggling to reach the tiny leaves at the top of the tree. "He needs some help," she thought, so she swooped down and plucked a few of the tenderest leaves for him.

When Portia gave Jeremy the leaves, his spots went pale with shame and embarrassment.

"I should be able to get those myself," he wailed. "Why won't my neck stretch?"

"Oh, Jeremy," said Portia, "your neck is just fine! It's still growing, that's all. Just keep eating your greens and getting lots of sleep, and it will grow!"

"But I can't wait," Jeremy insisted. "Isn't there anything I can do to make my neck long and stretchy now?"

"Perhaps there is," said Portia. "I think I know just the place to do it. Follow me, Jeremy!"

Portia led Jeremy through the jungle to a clearing.
Jeremy's eyes widened with wonder at what he saw.
There was so much going on!

Seymour Snake was wrapping himself round and round a fallen tree trunk. "Hello, Jeremy," he hissed.

" Jussssst doing

my sssssslithering exercisessssss!"

Nearby, Eric and Ellen, Elephant were hoisting heavy logs. "One, two, three, LIFT!" they chanted together.

"Hi, Jeremy!" called Eric. "We're just doing our trunk-strengthening workout."

Near the riverbank, Grandpa Gorilla was holding out thick branches for Claudia Crocodile to break in half.

"Just limbering up my jaw muscles," Claudia snapped.

Leonard Lion was taking his own cubs, Louis and Lisa, through their pouncing paces. "Welcome to the Jungle Gym, Jeremy!" he called.

A few minutes later, Grandpa Gorilla and Leonard Lion came to greet Jeremy. "What can we do for you?" they asked.

"My neck is too short," said Jeremy. "Can you help me stretch it? I want to be able to reach the tasty, tiny, tender leaves at the tops of the trees, just like my dad does."

"You're still growing," said Leonard Lion. "Just eat up all your greens, get lots of sleep, and your neck will grow."

Jeremy's face fell. But he brightened up when Grandpa Gorilla said, "In the meantime, we can give you a special program of neck-stretching exercises to help things along. Come with us!"

Grandpa got Jeremy started right away.

"S-t-r-e-t-c-h to the left!

S-t-r-e-t-c-h to the right!"

Grandpa Gorilla shouted.

"Chin lifts next," said Leonard Lion. Jeremy s-t-r-e-e-e-t-c-h-e-d as far as he could to get his chin onto the branch.

"Come on, you can do it!" Portia said, cheering him on.

"I think Seymour can help with the next one," said Grandpa Gorilla. "Jeremy, you get down on the ground, and Seymour — start slithering!"

"Aaaakkk!"

gasped Jeremy, as
Seymour wrapped himself
round his neck.

"Er... not quite so tight, Seymour," said
Grandpa.

"Aaaaahh!" sighed Jeremy. "That's better!"
Seymour slithered along, pu-u-u-l-l-ing
Jeremy's neck muscles as he went.

All the exercise made Jeremy really hungry. At supper that evening, he had three BIG helpings of greens.

He was tired, too, so he went to bed early and slept soundly all night.

Jeremy couldn't wait to get back to the Jungle Gym and do some more neck-stretching exercises. He went back the next day, the day after that, and the day after that.

"You're making excellent progress, Jeremy," Leonard Lion told him.

Every evening after his workout, Jeremy ate a good supper.

"Exercising makes me soooo hungry…" he told his mom and dad…

"and sOOOO

tired," he yawned, as he settled down to sleep.

A few days later, Jeremy and his dad went out leaf-gathering together. Suddenly, Jeremy spotted a brand-new bunch of succulent, sweet-looking leaves right at the top of a tall tree.

"I'm going to get those, Dad," he said.

"But Jeremy," said Dad, "they're so high up!"

Jeremy didn't hear him. He was too busy stretching… and

stre-e-e-e-e-tching…

and… s t r e e e t c h i n g…

…until he stretched right up to the very top branch!

"I've done it, Dad!" he cried happily. "The exercises worked!"

That night, Jeremy's mom and dad
made a super-special salad with the
leaves Jeremy had picked, and
they all enjoyed it together.

"Do you think it was the exercises,
Jeremy?" his dad asked. "Or has
your neck grown because of all
the greens you've been eating
and all the sleep you've been
getting?"

"I don't know," replied
Jeremy. "What do you
think, Mom?"

"I think it doesn't matter at all," replied Mom. "What matters is that you have a fine, strong,

lo-o-o-o-ng neck

that any giraffe would be proud of!"

"And I am!" said Jeremy, taking another mouthful of tasty, tender leaves. He chewed the leaves extra thoroughly — because he knew they had a very long way to go!

This is a Bright Sparks Book
This edition published in 2001
BRIGHT SPARKS, Queen Street House, 4 Queen Street, Bath BA1 1HE, UK

Copyright © PARRAGON 2000

Created and produced by THE COMPLETE WORKS,
St. Mary's Road, Royal Leamington Spa, Warwickshire CV31 1JP, UK

ISBN 0-84250-433-9

Printed in China